WHEN IT'S TIME TO POOP

written by MELANIE HOBUS   illustrated by SARAH LOWTHER

Copyright 2019 Melanie Hobus

https://website

All rights reserved. No part of this book may be used or reproduced by any means, graphic, electronic, or mechanical, including photocopying, recording, taping or by any information storage retrieval system without the written permission of the author except in the case of brief quotations embodied in critical articles and reviews.

Illustrations by Sarah Lowther

Edited by Phyllis Jask

Printed in the United States of America

ISBN-13: 978-0-578-58202-3

This book is dedicated to my daughter Raegan Hobus. Thanks to her, she made this idea come to life.

Raegan, you are a true blessing and a very special girl. We love you very much.

Now that I'm a big kid, I learned how to use the potty. At first I learned to pee, it was easy as...

Now it's time to learn to poop...

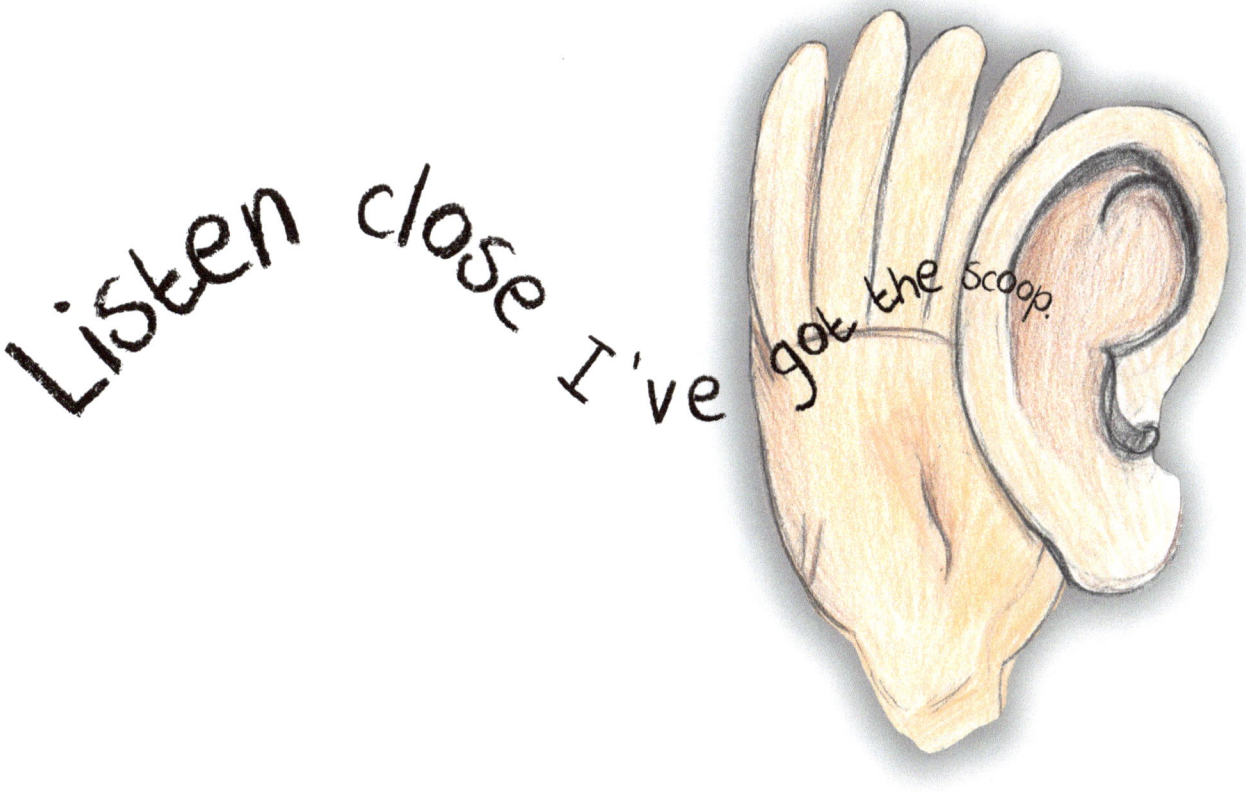

When you're busy or playing outside, swinging on swings, or sliding down slides, you have to STOP just for a minute; because if you don't, you'll be sitting in it! EWWW!

Accidents happen, and that's okay too. Just know, that we are still so proud of you!

Sometimes you need to have patience and it can take a while. But when it comes, you'll feel so good, we'll all clap hands and smile!

My favorite fruits to eat are peaches, pears, and plums. When my belly is full of them I say,

"Look out world here it comes!"

If you feel the poop
is on the way,
and you make
it to the potty,
it will be a great day.

Sometimes it helps to
jump it out,
push real hard,
or sing and shout.
Don't be afraid,
just let it out!

What's that you say?

"I POOPED!"

HIP HIP HOORAY!

Good job my sweetie, my dear, my love! We knew you could do it, let's all cheer and hug!

Melanie Hobus is a full time cosmetologist, wife, and mom. Even though hair and makeup are her passion, she has always loved the written word. Once Melanie and her husband became parents, they sought to teach their daughter as much as they could. Potty training was a pivotal teaching moment for the whole family. The words started flowing one night while trying to help their daughter Raegan use the potty. Inspired, Melanie put her words to paper, thinking her story could help other toddlers and their parents reach this milestone, just as it helped Raegan. Melanie's artistic sister Sarah created custom paintings for Raegan's nursery, and Melanie knew Sarah's talent would bring the book to life. Melanie and Sarah are very close, so to have created this book together is a gift beyond measure.

Sarah Lowther has a passion for creating art of all kinds. Her career has taken her on the road into the beauty industry, leading her to Hollywood's front door as a special effects hair and makeup artist. When Melanie asked her for help with illustrations for this book, Sarah embraced the opportunity to create art especially for her beloved niece. Sarah remains excited to be a part of this teaching milestone for all children.

Follow us on Facebook: whenitstimetopoop
Email: whenitstimetopoop@gmail.com

www.ingramcontent.com/pod-product-compliance
Lightning Source LLC
Chambersburg PA
CBHW041408160426
42811CB00103B/1553